WHEN I MAKE IT TO HEAVEN, I'M GOING STRAIGHT TO THE COMPLAINT DEPARTMENT

BY JOEL REED

LUCIDBOOKS

I would like to dedicate this book to my late wife, Jeanne V. Reed, and to my family.

INTRODUCTION

It's high time someone stepped up and made known to God what we know about the poor design and function of this otherwise marvelous and miraculous creation which we call the human body. I intend to take these grievances to the complaint department in heaven, assuming I make it there, of course.

A friend of mine asked me recently what my book was about. I told him the title: *When I Make It to Heaven, I'm Going Straight to the Complaint Department.* At first he laughed, but then he said "Complaint Department? What makes you think there is a complaint department in heaven?

Everything there is supposed to be heavenly. What could there be to complain about in heaven?"

I replied, "Certainly an organization as big as heaven has a place where people can express their concerns. It's not actually to complain about heaven, it's for things that could be better here on earth. Most big corporations have something like this; they probably changed the name to customer service or customer relations but that amounts to the same thing.

After all, complaints are nothing new. In the British Museum, there is writing on a clay tablet dated to around 1,700 BC about someone who received a poorer grade of ore than they were promised. It's a complaint: a 4,000-year-old complaint. In any event, I want to make my problems—things of a medical nature I think should be corrected—known to God. I am pretty sure He could have done a better job and He still has time to make the proper corrections."

My friend stopped laughing and wished me "Good luck!"

The Time Arrives

St. Peter: Joel, welcome to heaven.

Joel: Oh my God! Am I really here? Oops, maybe I shouldn't say that up here.

St. Peter: You're here all right, and I'm here to welcome you and show you around. We usually give a little time for newcomers to get oriented, but I'm told yours is a special case. I hear that you want to go "straight to the complaint department." Unfortunately, we don't really have a complaint department, not by that or any other name. We've, actually, never had a complaint before. But, Joel, God already knows of your desire to talk and He has decided He will take care of it Himself. He is waiting for you right now.

Joel: Oh my God!

St. Peter: That's Him. You look a little nervous. Are you frightened?

Joel: That is not the half of it. I am terrified, I think I just wet my pants.

St. Peter: Calm down, Joel. God is just as understanding as you might expect and He is anxious to hear your complaints.

Joel: St. Peter, could we maybe stop calling them complaints? They're more like questions that puzzle me as a doctor. I'm afraid complaint is too strong a word.

St. Peter: Call it whatever you want, God isn't offended. He's ready to hear what you have to say. I'll take you there now. I can show you around later.

Joel: I'm still worried about calling it the complaint department. It seems too aggressive.

St. Peter: He knows.

Joel: I really am in such awe of Him. I'm afraid I'll clam up.

St. Peter: He knows.

Joel: I hope he already knows how I feel about His creation of the earth, of the heavens, of the universe, and how I feel especially in awe of the human body. What a wonder it is.

I have to admit, when I was in school and then in college, enrolled in science courses like chemistry, anatomy, physiology, or biology, I felt like I knew the answers to so many mysteries of life. I understood how atoms combine to form molecules, and how those combine to form even more complex compounds, and how those combine to form even more complex combinations. It was easy to imagine the next step, how these compounds, together in a muddy pool on a primitive earth, stimulated by outside energy like a nearby lightning strike, could become a simple form of life.

St. Peter: Well, He'll be happy to hear that you're a fan of his work…

Joel: But then, when I got into medical school and learned a little more about all of this, I realized just how complex even the simplest form of life was. The odds against life being able to exist by chance are astronomical. It's totally unreasonable.

If you have any doubts about that, look at the structure of DNA. When I learned about DNA, the key to life, and I saw how each of the chemicals in that helix is arranged in a precise pattern, that's all I needed to know to understand that there was more than random chance at work. This was genius beyond human comprehension. Look at it and just try to tell me you think that could happen by a chance combination of atoms.

St. Peter: Well, everyone here is pretty positive God had something to do with it…

Joel: Number crunchers have studied the probability. One time, I read an excerpt from Stephen Meyer that said, "Run the odds of these things falling into place on their own and you find that the probabilities of forming a rather short functional protein at random would be one chance in a hundred thousand trillion trillion trillion trillion trillion trillion trillion trillion trillion. That's a ten with 125 zeroes behind it!"[1] There's no way it could happen. So, I became a firm believer in intelligent design. Only God could do this.

St. Peter: He already knows all that. He knows

---

1. Stephen Meyer, *Signature in the Cell: DNA and the Evidence for Intelligent Design* (New York: HarperOne, 2010), quoted in Mark Mittelberg, *The Questions Christians Hope No One Will Ask (with Answers)* (Carol Stream, IL: Tyndale House Publishers, 2010), 40.

how it works. He knows how you found out. He knows how committed you are to your beliefs. He knows it all. He's God, that's His thing. You're nervous, I understand. But we're here now so just relax and when you meet Him just say what's on your mind.

Joel: Hang on, I need just a moment to catch my breath and muster up some courage…

Okay, I guess I'm as ready as I'll ever be. Let's go.

St. Peter: Hello, God, I hope we haven't kept you waiting. Joel is here to talk with you.

God: Thank you, Peter. Joel, take a seat and make yourself comfortable. Why don't you tell me what's on your mind?

Joel: God, I guess you know how nervous I am. I was worried about how to approach these things. I've been referring to them as complaints, which is a little harsh, when actually they're more like problems I've had with understanding. I'm a physician and I've had trouble dealing with the way certain organs work or, better yet, the way they don't work exactly how I think they should.

It's a pretty long list and I know you must be very busy. I don't want to take up too much of your time.

God: I want to hear what you have to say. Don't worry about the time. We don't measure time here the way that you're used to on earth. Here we have eternity.

Joel: Well, at first I was worried about where to start, but I have a patient who has suffered repeated difficulties with…umm…a particular body part. He begged me to put it at the top of my list. Neither of us could figure out why you would have included it in the first place. We were both quite frustrated. There was little I could do to prevent recurrences or even to relieve his symptoms. He had itching, burning, even bleeding on occasion. I treated him with every salve or ointment I could think of, even suppositories and hot sitz baths. Surgical removal could give some long-term relief, but that was a last resort. It includes a lot of pain even if the surgery itself is minor.

I believe you know precisely what problem I'm describing. God, where in the world did you come up with hemorrhoids? I must have seen hundreds, or even thousands of patients suffering from them, yet they seem to have little function and we could easily do without them. Please, don't make these patients wait through the slow process of evolution. Perform a miracle and get rid of hemorrhoids. You would make a lot of people happy.

God: I like to think I already make a lot of people happy. You make a good point though. I'm going to give that problem some serious consideration. Do you have more?

Joel: I'm just getting started. I know I'm taking a lot of your time and I appreciate your listening to me. Would it be better if I came back at another time to tell you more?

God: Remember, here in heaven we don't think of time like that. What may seem like a long time to you isn't even a second compared to eternity. Go on. I'm interested in hearing everything you have to say.

Joel: You're so gracious. It had originally been my intention to start with sinuses, paranasal sinuses specifically. Here again, I saw hundreds, even thousands of people suffering from what I'm sure were unintended consequences of their creation. I'm sure you had a good reason for including them.

Most doctors, myself included, suspect you made them to lighten the skull which is already quite heavy. It does need to be strong to protect the delicate brain. Its weight, however, puts strain on the neck and so many people have neck pain because of this. But, the sinuses have one main drawback: The lining is the same as in the nasal passages. The slightest irritation from pollen, smoke, or pollution causes swelling, and then the drainage from the sinus is blocked. Mucus collects and infection follows. The patient feels pain, pressure, headache, and has difficulty breathing. Treating the infection is nearly worthless since the underlying problem is the inadequate drainage. It could be so easily improved if you would only increase the size of the drainage openings or put them in a better place so that gravity would help keep the mucus flowing. Can't you work on this?

I'm beginning to worry about how much of your time I'm taking. Should I go on or schedule another time?

God: As I told you before, don't be concerned about time. We have an eternity and you are making some good points.

Joel: You are unquestionably as kind and patient and loving as I was told you would be.

God: I am. I know.

Joel: God, I hope you'll forgive my strong language, but I cannot think of a better way to put this. I'm afraid to tell you that your design of the human back is an unmitigated disaster! It may have been fine for walking around on all fours. That must be where it started. Slowly, through evolution, you eventually got us to upright, but you didn't make the changes needed for the back to function well in this position.

The design is bad, and evolution isn't getting the job done. Even simple procedures such as bending over to pick something up can cause enough pain to put someone in bed for days. We try to bend our knees, to let the legs do most of the work and we try not to lift weights that are heavier than we should, but if we do very much of this, it can lead to permanent disability. We wear out our joints and the discs in our backs. Almost all the joints in our bodies wear out too quickly. Calcium builds up and can pinch nerves or result in weakness or loss of sensation. And people who go too far to the other end of the spectrum, who are inactive or don't do any heavy work or exercise, suffer a softening of the bones called osteoporosis. The bones get so soft they just collapse under normal weight and activity. Believe me, that's a painful condition and takes a long time to heal.

It's clear to me that the back needs a complete redesign.

Surely there are engineers here in heaven who could help with a redesign because, believe me, it is sorely needed. A friend of mine from the University of Texas says you must have used graduates from Texas A&M. He was kidding, of course. At least I think he was.

We have very able surgeons who can work wonders to relieve some of the pain when nerves are compressed or damaged, but all they can do is treat the symptoms. The underlying causes of the trouble still exist. Patients expect to be made well again but that isn't possible.

God, please do something and don't make us wait any longer on evolution.

God: Hmm...

Joel: If you are ready, I have got more.

God: Bring them on.

Joel: This next one is big. It concerns our gastrointestinal tract. It plainly is not designed for today's diet, if you can even call it that.

God: I'm going to stop you right there. Your gastrointestinal tract is designed for the food I intended for you. It does a perfectly acceptable job digesting fruits, vegetables, and nuts.

Joel: But we wanted better tasting, richer foods. We learned how to produce sugar from cane and from beets and from a bunch of other sources. We add it to almost everything and eat so much more because it tastes so great.

God: Free will, Joel. That was the deal. I gave you an abundance of wholesome healthy foods, but you have the free will to choose the other things that are bad for you.

Joel: But it's resulting in obesity, even morbid obesity. It's an epidemic. Can't you make it less sweet, maybe even bitter? Just do something to stop us from pigging out and destroying ourselves.

God: That's not how free will works, Joel. You all just need to practice a little self-restraint.

Joel: What about meat? Meat's another problem.

God: Meat was never a part of the plan at first. They didn't eat meat in Eden, you know. You're not equipped with the claws or fangs needed to tear flesh from another animal.

Joel: But we learned that if we cook the meat, that makes it edible and delicious. It works best if it has plenty of fat, but all that fat pushes our cholesterol level up so high it damages our blood vessels or causes heart attacks or strokes.

God: It sounds like you'll just have to exercise some of that free will I gave you to eat a little better.

Joel: Even if we ate only the foods you intended for us, there is an unintended consequence which we find very embarrassing. These foods promote the formation of gas. It has to get out one way or another, and when it does, it makes a distinctive sound. We call it a fart. For some reason when that happens, everyone laughs.

God: Of course they start laughing. It's funny.

Joel: It is decidedly embarrassing. Sometimes

it happens in a crowded elevator, or worse yet, in church. You try to do it soundlessly or to hope the sound is drowned out by a loud hymn. That's just half the battle. Even if you can let it out with no one noticing, there's no escaping the odor. Your only defense is to look at someone else and hope people think it came from them.

God: You mean like a lie? I think I've made it pretty clear how I feel about that.

Joel: Can't you just make them stop? At least get rid of the odor. Something needs to change. What possible use could there be for farts? God, May I tell you a story that shows how funny farts can be?

God: Of course, if you keep it clean.

Joel: This is a good one. Stop me if you've already heard it. There was a young boy who wasn't doing well in school. His parents did everything they could to help, hiring tutors, helping him with his homework, but nothing seemed to work. He continued to do poorly. Then, one day, he comes home and throws out his chest and proudly announces that he answered a question correctly in school that day. His parent praised him and told him how proud they were and then they asked him what the question was.

He replied, "Who farted?"

God: Haha! That's a good story. Go on, tell me your next point.

Joel: I've got a big problem with the urinary tract. Not personally, I mean the urinary tract is problematic, especially for men but for some women too. Everything starts out working well, but as they age, men begin to notice a slower, smaller stream. It takes longer and longer to empty their bladders and after a while they have to use more and more force. This is because of an enlarged prostate, which already has a pretty high risk of cancer. Is there any way you can stop this growth and build up resistance to cancer here. Maybe consider moving the gland so that it doesn't interfere with urination anymore.

God: That's an interesting thought…

Joel: And while we're talking about that area, what in the world were you thinking when you commanded Solomon to circumcise himself and all the males in his family? You know it's a Jewish tradition now, don't you? They call it a *Brit Milah* or *Bris*. All Jewish boys are circumcised on the eighth day after their birth.

I don't see how Christianity could have spread as far and as fast as it did if they had to do this the way Jewish men do. You know, some of them are actually doing it for supposed "medical" reasons, but there's very little evidence of any health benefits.

Joel: That reminds me of another funny story. May I tell it?

God: Surely, same rules though.

Joel: A man was admitted to the hospital and is waiting in his room before surgery. His roommate turns to him and asks "What are you in for?" He says, "I just here for a circumcision." His roommate looks at him, aghast, and asks if the doctor had explained all of the complications. He said that the doctor had made a few jokes but told him that he could go home right after the procedure was completed. The roommate shook his head gravely and said "That's not what happened to me. I was circumcised when I was eight days old and I didn't walk for a year!"

God: Ha!

Joel: Can I tell you another funny story?

God: Go ahead. You have some good ones.

Joel: There was a young couple out to dinner with their five-year-old son. About halfway through the meal, the lad leans over to his mother and says "Mommy, I have to pee-pee." She turns to him and says, "You're a big boy now. You can go by yourself," and she points to the restroom door a few feet away and tells him she'll be watching for him until he's done.

Now, this was the first time he had ever gone to a public restroom by himself, and he was anxious, but he mustered his courage and went in. Quite a while goes by and his mommy is getting worried. So, she gets up from her chair and, just then, the restroom door is flung open and the child comes out with his pants all wet, crying loudly.

"What happened in there that upset you so much?" she asks.

He says, "I got behind two old men. One couldn't get started, the other couldn't stop, and I couldn't wait."

And, God, that's what happens when men get older.

God: Not bad!

Joel: Women have their own difficulties, though. The female urethra is short making them far more susceptible to infections. After childbirth, the muscles and tissues that support the bladder are stretched and the lack of support can result in leakage. At first only with cough or strain, but it can advance until it's almost continuously leaking.

God: Hey, that's part and parcel to the whole "pain in childbirth" deal I made with Eve.

Joel: The point is, things aren't great down there for men or for women. Your help is really needed. But I have a few more things to go over.

Joel: God, I see so many patients with high blood-pressure or diabetes or both who are completely unaware that they have these problems.

These are very serious illnesses and they can be life threatening. Sometimes people are completely without symptoms until it's too late. We call them "silent killers." If you could only assign some pain to them at an early stage, a little pain for mild disease, maybe increasing in intensity as the conditions get worse. You don't even have to make them go away, just something that would get the patient's attention before any serious damage is done.

God: If people just scheduled regular check-ups, it would be discovered at an early stage when you could still do something about it.

Joel: Well, now that my courage is up a little, I'll start letting loose on you, okay? Again, I ask that you forgive my forcefulness, but you really goofed…

God: Goofed?

Joel: Yes, goofed. You really goofed when you created mosquitoes, flies, and cockroaches. I don't know if you've had time to keep track of everything that's happening on earth, but you should know that mosquitoes cause more human suffering and loss of life than any other organism. Worldwide, more than a million people die from diseases transmitted by this little devil every year.[2]

They transmit a host of diseases like malaria, chikungunya virus, canine heart worms, dengue and yellow fever, encephalitis, West Nile virus, and Zika.[3] What a list! Mosquitoes are much worse than an irritating pest. They are a serious threat to the life and health of millions of people each year. What purpose did you have in creating them? How could you create such a monster? I think the least you could do is show us an effective way to eliminate them.

---

2. "Mosquito-Borne Diseases," The American Mosquito Control Association, accessed April 11, 2017, http://www.mosquito.org/mosquito-borne-diseases.

3. Ibid.

God: Okay, no mosquitoes…

Joel: And house flies, another goof in the same vein. They transmit as many as 65 diseases to humans alone: typhoid fever, dysentery, cholera, poliomyelitis, yaws, anthrax, tularemia, leprosy, and tuberculosis.[4]

God: Okay, mosquitoes and house flies…

Joel: And that's not the end! Cockroaches! Cockroaches eat everything, go everywhere, and love warm places like inside a home. Their favorite place is food preparation areas and they spread bacteria like *pseudomonas aeruginosa*.[5] That is one bad bug, resistant to most antibiotics.

Joel: I haven't even mentioned tobacco yet. It is a scourge on our people. The plant is not particularly pretty and it's not known for its beautiful blooms. The only reason we keep it around is for the nicotine in its leaves. That is one powerfully addicting drug.

---

4. Steve Jacobs Sr., "House Flies," accessed April 11, 2017, http://ento.psu.edu/extension/factsheets/house-flies.

5. K. Saitou, K. Furuhata, Y. Kawakami, M. Fukuyama, "Isolation of Pseudomonas aeruginosa from Cockroaches Captured in Hospitals in Japan, and Their Antibiotic Susceptibility," accessed April 11, 2017, https://www.ncbi.nlm.nih.gov/pubmed/20055220.

It takes just a few days of use, smoking or chewing or sniffing, to become hopelessly addicted. I've treated cocaine addicts who said it was easier to kick their cocaine habit than nicotine. People seem to think that it makes them look sophisticated or "cool," but it does exactly the opposite. By the time they realize that, it's usually too late. They're already addicted. Can't you make that plant extinct?

God: Alright! I might be a being of infinite patience and mercy, but my feelings can still be hurt. I feel like you have left out an important consideration. You are pointing your finger right at me to fix all of these problems. My question is: "Have you given any consideration to what part the devil may have played in any of this?"

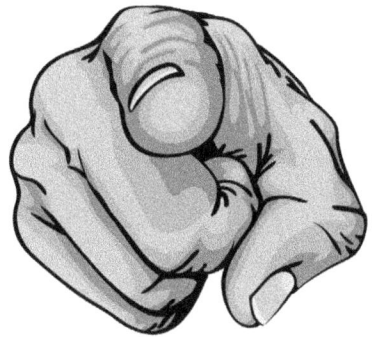

Joel: I never really bought into that idea. The image of the devil is as a little man dressed in red with a pitchfork and a pointed tail never seemed realistic to me.

God: You and me both, but that doesn't mean he doesn't exist. He is like a lion waiting to devour you. He speaks to you like a little voice inside of you, tempting you to do those things that will give you immediate pleasure. It's him tempting you to eat those foods that taste good instead of the ones that are good for you. It's him tempting you to eat fatty cooked meats. He tempts you to engage in all kinds of risky behaviors that will be bad for you in the long run. He's the cause of your obesity, your vascular and heart disease, and your back and joint pain. Are you saying he has never tempted you to do these things?

Joel: Well, no, he's tempted me many times

every day. I guess I've never looked at it in that way. I was focusing on the miracles I thought you should perform here on earth. I guess I just thought with such formidable powers you could simply eliminate all these sources of pain and suffering. You raised Lazarus, you restored sight to the blind, you cured the paralytic at the pool, cured the lepers and so many other miracles. Can you understand why I would think you should use those same powers everywhere for everyone? Many people think that because these problems exist here on earth, that you must not exist. They think that if you did, there would be only peace, love, and good health. But, I guess that is the new heaven and new earth described in Revelation 21.

God: Joel, you may recall that I specifically performed those miracles to show people who I really am and the powers I possess. In far more cases, I simply gave them the strength to confront and manage their troubles. Better yet, to focus on the divine, the spiritual life. I tried to inspire the resistance of temptation and how to focus on the eternal during my own human experience. For 40 days in the wilderness I prepared myself to confront the devil face to face. I refused to use my power to relieve my own hunger or to protect myself from harm. I refused to be drawn in by human desire for riches or fame or power. That was not to be my kingdom. Chasing after those goals leads to a dead end.

Joel: Okay, God. I understand that performing a miracle might not be the answer, but surely you could have steered evolution to alleviate some of these problems?

God: I know you've had some complaints about the slow process of evolution. Try to keep in mind how much shorter your lifetimes are compared with the time table for evolution. It takes millions of earth years for a species to evolve. Think of the discovery of the "Ice Man."

Joel: The "Ice Man?" You mean the one discovered in the Alps between Italy and Switzerland?

God: Exactly. His body was frozen and protected

from the elements for over 5,000 years. I'm sure you must have seen it on TV. Scientists did a forensic reconstruction. Had they dressed him in modern clothes, he could have walked around and no one would be able to tell the difference. Even 5,000 years later human beings still look the same. Trust me, it would be chaos if evolution moved any faster than it does. In heavenly time, it's right on schedule.

Joel: I guess that makes sense.

God: Joel, do you remember what Matthew said of my temptation in the desert?

Joel: Of course. After 40 days and nights, I can't for a moment imagine how hungry you must have been.

God: I was famished. My body cried out for nourishment, but I quoted Scripture to Satan: *"Man shall not live on bread alone, but on every word that comes from the mouth of God"* (Matt. 4:4). I would not use my power to satisfy my own wants and needs.

That didn't stop him. He then took me to the pinnacle of the temple in Jerusalem. He tried quoting Scripture at me but I responded from Deuteronomy, *"You shall not put the LORD your God to the test"* (Deut. 6:16). I would not use my power to save myself from pain, suffering, or death.

Lucifer still would not give up and took me to the top of a mountain and offered me all the kingdoms of the earth if I would just worship him.

Joel: I think I understand what you're saying, God. His temptation draws us to eat too much or to eat things that taste good rather than the things which are good for us. This is why so many of us are obese or have high blood pressure, diabetes, or heart disease. He tempts us to abuse our bodies either with a sedentary lifestyle or by over exerting ourselves. Our muscles and bones become weak or we wear out our joints and then we look to you or to medicine to cure us. But how can we avoid this temptation when he overwhelms our intellect and forethought and we lose focus on what is really important?

God: You must do as I did. I simply said, "Away from me, Satan! For it is written: *Worship the Lord your God, and serve Him only*" (Matt. 4:10). Where I have not used my power to cure you, I have promised that I would walk with you through any adversity.

Joel: You have opened my eyes, God. The temptations of unhealthy choices may be easier or bring us pleasure in the moment, but they expose us to greater risk and misfortune in the future. I see now that with your guidance and help, we can face temptation and conquer any trials.

God: I sent you a patient to try and teach you that lesson. Do you remember him?

Joel: I think I know who you're talking about, and I still think of him almost daily, even though that happened so many years ago.

God: Tell me what you can remember of him.

Joel: I don't recall his exact age, but he was in his mid-20's. He had been diving into a shallow pool and crushed the vertebra in his neck, severing his spinal cord and leaving him paralyzed from the neck down. I'd seen patients with this injury before. They're extremely prone to infection due to the loss of feeling and muscle control.

Since his injury, he had been repeatedly hospitalized with pneumonia or infections;

sometimes one episode would begin just as another was clearing up.

One day, during one of his stays in the hospital, I made a routine visit to his room during my morning rounds. I found him moved to a sitting position with the bedside table pulled up in front of him like a desk. He had a headset on and a phone was resting on the table. I tried to excuse myself but he insisted I stay. "What's happening here?" I asked once he finished his call. He responded, "I work as a telemarketer so that I can support my family." He and his wife were both people of strong faith. Despite all their trials, they continued to work hard and keep smiles on their faces. Tears welled up in my eyes. I had never seen anything like that in all the years I had been practicing medicine. Because you gave him the strength to believe that, eventually, everything would be alright, he and his wife were able to confront his severe impairment and still remain productive and happy. I try to never use the word "disabled," preferring instead "physically impaired." Disability only occurs when one focuses on what one has lost instead of living with what one has.

I'll bet it was you again who directed me to

visit the Brookwood Community right here in Brookshire, Texas. I'm certain you know of it. They keep an empty chair in each room designated as "God's chair." The "citizens" of that community, as they are called, suffer some of the most profound physical impairments you can imagine. Some have severe forms of brain damage from various causes, Down syndrome and other genetic conditions, and many types of bodily injuries. Yet, not a single one of them is "disabled" in the usual sense. Each of them has a job tailored to their abilities. They are happy. I've never seen so many smiles. I could see you at work in each of their lives. From that time forward, I was reassured that my refusal to use the word disabled was correct. People are not disabled unless they let themselves be. I feel sorry for those with physical impairments who do not know you and do not know they can call upon you for strength so that they can follow this path. Since then, I can see you at work in my daily life.

God: Remember that I showed you how to remain focused on the things that are really important and how your faith can help you overcome temptation.

Joel: I must admit, God, that throughout my life I have struggled with my faith. I have at times had strong faith, but at others I have almost totally rejected my faith. I have looked for answers in the Scripture. It was your apostle, John, who recorded your words in the 10th chapter of his gospel: *"I and the Father are one"* (John 10:30). *"If you really know me you will know my Father as well"* (John 14:7).

And of course, I recall his words *"God is love"* (1 John 4:8). You, indeed, are love. When we let you into our lives and let you be our guide, we can be exceptionally happy. No obstacle, physical impairment, or other type of failure will be able to conquer us. You will be there to give us strength and hope. Managing it will be easy.

Even knowing all of this, I will admit there are parts of my faith that I have always struggled with. The concept of the Trinity—the Father, Son, and Holy Spirit—has always been hard for me to fully grasp. It has made me wonder if the claims that we worship three Gods are right.

God: Maybe a visual example will help. Imagine a clear glass full of water. When you look at that glass, you imagine you can see the water inside of it, right? Wrong! The water and even the glass are both transparent and therefore invisible. What you're actually seeing is the effect they have on the light around them. The water in that glass that you can't see is like me, invisible but affecting all the world around you. What would happen if the temperature were dropped below freezing?

Joel: I imagine that water would turn into ice.

God: Exactly. The water would become ice which you can see and feel and interact with but would remain the same water as before. This is like Jesus. Now, what would happen if the temperature of the water was raised; what if it became quite warm?

Joel: I guess it would melt and begin to evaporate.

God: Precisely. The water turns into vapor in the atmosphere. A different form, and no more visible to you, but still there.

Joel: I think I understand now. The same water can be vapor in the air, liquid in a glass, or frozen solid in ice. The Trinity is the same way: Father, Son, and Holy Spirit, all the same water, so to speak.

God: Good, I'm glad you understand. You know, Joel, I can see that you got the messages I was trying to give to you. You have conducted your life and treated your patients well. I don't blame you for at least being led astray. Doubts can actually strengthen your faith. Many feel that I should use my powers to eliminate all suffering on earth. You're not alone in that. But you must remember that my kingdom is not of the world. It's spiritual in nature.

You have done well to not be tempted by the earthly, but now it's time for you to learn a little more about the spiritual world, heaven. I am going to call Peter and ask him to show you around now. He'll give you some idea of what heaven is all about. You have many friends here anxious to see you. One of my Special Angels, who has always been known for her infinite patience, is actually becoming impatient to see you.

The End

www.ingramcontent.com/pod-product-compliance
Lightning Source LLC
Chambersburg PA
CBHW041142170626
46815CB00007B/345